This Book Belongs to:

Halloween
Is It for Real?

Harold Myra

ILLUSTRATED BY JANE KURISU

Tommy
NELSON®

Thomas Nelson, Inc.
Nashville

Copyright © 1979, 1997 by Harold Myra

Illustrations copyright © 1997 by Tommy Nelson®, a division of Thomas Nelson, Inc.

Published in Nashville, Tennessee, by Tommy Nelson®, a division of Thomas Nelson, Inc.

Scripture quotation is from the *International Children's Bible, New Century Version*,
copyright © 1986, 1988, 1999 by Tommy Nelson®, a division of Thomas Nelson, Inc.

Library of Congress Cataloging-in-Publication Data

Myra, Harold Lawrence, 1939–

    Halloween, is it for real? / Harold Myra : illustrated by Jane Kurisu.
      p. cm.
    Summary: Teaches a Christian view of Halloween by presenting it as a holiday on which
to celebrate God's victory over evil and evil spirits.
     ISBN 0-8499-1494-9
     1. Halloween—Juvenile literature. [1. Halloween.]   I. Kurisu, Jane, 1952–   ill.
II. Title.
GT4965.M93   1997   97-20393
394.2646—dc21   CIP
                                                          AC

Printed in the United States of America

02 03 04 PHX 9 8 7 6

A Note to Parents

Halloween is an odd mixture of creepy
creatures, costume parties, and harvest
festivals. It is a confusing holiday for
Christians.

Should parents encourage the celebration
of a holiday that traces its roots to pagan
practices and beliefs?

The challenge for Christian parents is to
teach our children to use this holiday to
celebrate God's victory over evil and evil
spirits. It is my hope that this book will
help.

—Harold Myra

Todd grinned as he held up a Halloween mask with a mangled face and scary eyes.

Greg sneaked a hairy fake tarantula onto Mom's arm.

"This Halloween," Todd announced, "I'm going to make a monster room with bloody bones and peeled grapes for eyeballs."

"Yuck!" said Michelle. "Why do people love this stuff anyway?"

"Because it's cool!" Todd answered.

"But why does anyone celebrate Halloween?" Michelle asked.

"I've heard that it is called the devil's holiday," Todd said.

"It all started long ago, before Christ was born," Dad explained. "People believed that a lord of death sent evil spirits into animals to play terrible tricks on people. To escape them, people wore disguises."

"Is that how wearing scary costumes started?" Michelle asked.

"Sure. And that's how playing pranks on Halloween got started too. Another tradition that got started then is the bonfire. People built huge bonfires to scare the pranksters away."

"Sounds like fun," Greg said.

"Not really! People died in cruel ceremonies."

Michelle grimaced. "Is that what Halloween means then?
Horrible evening or something?"

"Just the opposite," said Dad. "Christians tried to change the holiday into a festival of joy. October 31 became All Hallows' Eve. *All Hallows* means 'all holies' or 'all the saints.'"

"I thought Halloween was all about ghosts," Greg objected.

"It's about people who have died," said Mom. "But saints aren't ghosts. They're alive with Jesus, who rose from the dead and has a real body. We can celebrate!"

So celebrate they did. On October 31, Michelle, Todd, and Greg invited their friends, and the backyard was filled with kids in all sorts of costumes.

Later, jammed into the family room for cider,
caramel apples, and popcorn, Michelle started telling her
friends about All Hallows' Eve.

"It's our time to remember Grandma and Grandpa.
They're not really dead. They're alive with Jesus."

"My grandma died last year," a girl said. "She taught me a lot about Jesus."

"We miss our loved ones," Mom said. "But they're not sad. They're happy in a different world."

"We'll join them someday if we know Jesus, for he has conquered the forces of death and evil," said Dad.

Before going home, everyone sang "Amazing Grace":

When we've been there ten thousand years
Bright shining as the sun,
We've no less days to sing God's praise
Than when we'd first begun.

That night Greg said, "I still get scared. When I'm trying to get to sleep, the plant in my room looks like a monster."

"And sometimes I get bad dreams," said Todd.

Michelle asked, "Mom, how come we still like scary stories and movies, no matter how much we believe in Jesus?"

"Most stories are told in fun," said Mom. "But there is a supernatural world.

"Evil spirits do exist. And temptations."

"A lot of awful things happen in this world. Evil powers are nothing to fool around with! But the Bible teaches us that

'God did not give us a spirit that makes us afraid. He gave us a spirit of power and love.'

(2 TIMOTHY 1:7)

If you memorize the verse, you can say it to yourself when you get scared," said Dad.

After they all went to bed, gusty winds rattled the windows and made scary noises outside. But Michelle, Todd, and Greg snuggled under their warm blankets and smiled.

They talked to Jesus about their thoughts and hoped next Halloween would be as much fun as this one!